O'Dwy...

STARRING IN

ACTING INNOCENT

Heyes, Eileen.
O'Dwyer & Grady starring
in Acting innocent /
2002.
33305202493171
GI   08/09/02

O'Dwyer & Grady

STARRING IN

ACTING INNOCENT

By Eileen Heyes

New York   ingapore

SANTA CLARA COUNTY LIBRARY

3 3305 20249 3171

This book is a work of fiction. Any references to historical
events, real people, or real locales are used fictitiously.
Other names, characters, places, and incidents are the
product of the author's imagination, and any resem-
blance to actual events or locales or persons, living or
dead, is entirely coincidental.

If you purchased this book without a cover you should
be aware that this book is stolen property. It was
reported as "unsold and destroyed" to the publisher,
and neither the author nor the publisher has received
any payment for this "stripped book."

First Aladdin Paperbacks edition April 2002
Copyright © 2002 by Eileen Heyes

Aladdin Paperbacks
An imprint of Simon & Schuster
Children's Publishing Division
1230 Avenue of the Americas
New York, NY 10020

All rights reserved, including the right of reproduction
in whole or in part in any form.

Designed by Lisa Vega
The text of this book was set in Bembo

Printed and bound in the United States of America
10 9 8 7 6 5 4 3 2 1

The Library of Congress Control Number 2001041254

ISBN 0-689-84911-7

To my dad, William Heyes, Jr., the real-life Billy

CHAPTER ONE

I wasn't really naked. It was just supposed to
look that way.

If I'd really been naked, the bruise on
my leg and the thumbprint-size one above
my left elbow would have shown. But they
had me in this full-body pinkish leotard
thing. The prop guy picked me up, and I
grabbed the meat hook and hung there, and
then he pulled a mesh bag up from my feet
and looped it over the hook, too. "There
you go, Bill," he said. "You look just like a
side of beef."

Behind me, I could hear him back off
the set.

"Okay, places everyone!" That was the assistant director. A jerk, if you ask me. Nobody asked me.

I heard the familiar sounds of a scene being launched. The smack of the chalkboard that said what take we were on (nine, argh). The director's voice ordering: "Lights. Camera. And—action." Then the heavy footsteps of the two other actors. And their dialogue:

"All right, where's the kid?"

"He's right in here."

The scene was supposed to be taking place inside one of those big walk-in meat lockers at a restaurant, see, and the cook was hiding me. In an earlier scene, the cook had wrapped me up in a big fur coat that was hanging just inside the door, and one of these guys had found me. Now they stomped over to the coat, and one of them flung it open.

"There he—hey! Where did he go?" More stomping, and the two of them rushed back out of the meat locker.

"Cut!" A bell rang; my shoulders ached. "Okay, everybody, I think we can live with that one. Somebody get Billy down."

The prop guy, Joe, lifted me off the meat hook and helped me out of the mesh sack. I plopped myself onto a hard wooden chair, the nearest seat I could find. A second later, I felt big, warm hands massaging my shoulders.

"Some great acting there, Pardner. You had me convinced."

Surprised, I looked behind me and grinned. "Hiya, Roscoe," I said. "How come you're still here? I thought you'd finished your retakes."

"I have." He smiled back at me. "I just thought you might need a little shoulder rub after all that hanging."

That's the kind of guy he is. Roscoe "Chubby" Muldoon was my costar, or I was his, and he was the best pal I'd ever had. He had been one of the great comedians in the silent movies. I was only six in 1927, when the studios started putting sound in their pictures and Roscoe kind of disappeared for a while. But even though I was little, I remember my dad taking me to see all of the Chubby Muldoon pictures. Not in our wackiest dreams did we imagine I might actually work beside him, but here I was playing an abandoned kid in Roscoe's first talkie. He played the cook who was trying to protect me. My dad was thrilled, and so was I. When I first met Roscoe, he'd told me he liked to be called by his real name, so that's what I always called him.

"Well, Pardner"—and that's what he always called me—"I need to be going. Do you have many more scenes to reshoot?"

"Two or three, I think."

"That could take all day." He paused, an arm across my shoulders. "How about we have a day on the boardwalk after everything's wrapped up? I could use a nice greasy hot dog and some cotton candy. Tomorrow, let's say?"

"That'll be swell, Roscoe." I jumped out of my chair and gave him a hug. Yeah, I know it sounds babyish, me being eleven and all. I wouldn't have acted that way with anyone else at the studio, though.

"All right, see you around, Pardner." He ruffled my hair and walked away.

As I watched him head toward the soundstage exit, I heard the always irritating voice of Warren Hill, the jerk assistant director.

"Where's Chubby going in such a hurry?"

"It's Wednesday," Joe answered.

"And—? Oh, yeah. His little midweek errand."

He meant bootleg. Even though it was supposed to be illegal to buy liquor because of Prohibition, everyone seemed to have a way to get it. Most of the movie people I knew had theirs delivered, but Roscoe went every Wednesday to pick up his own whiskey.

While I sat there enjoying the feel of blood returning to my fingers, my manager, Maureen, marched out from the dark behind the cameras. A girl about my age walked beside her. I hadn't known Maureen was there; she usually doesn't stick around while we shoot. My stomach knotted. Maureen is the one who gave me those bruises on my leg and arm, but you'd never guess that from the way she acted at the studio.

"Hello, Mrs. Fritz," I said with a cheery smile. See, this is why my name's on all those marquees: I can act, real good.

"Well, hello, Billy," she said, just as cheery. It's a talent we share. "I want you to meet someone. This is Virginia Grady. She's going to play Fred in the *Rusty and Fred* pictures."

That was my next project—six comedies about a group of kids getting into mischief. I was going to play Rusty, the leader, and the Fred character was supposed to be a tomboy named Winifred who kept trying to get us boys to let her join us. This girl didn't look very tomboy at the moment. She wore a prim, light blue dress, and her shiny auburn hair, a couple shades darker than my own carrottop, fell without a tangle behind her shoulders. I was suddenly aware of how goofy I must have looked standing there in that leotard.

Maureen's voice took on a note of grandness as she continued, "Virginia, this is Billy O'Dwyer." She always introduces me like I'm the greatest star ever. What I am is her meal ticket.

"Hello, Virginia." I stuck out my hand for a shake, better trained than a monkey and trying to maintain my dignity.

"Hello, Billy." She did the same, her eyes looking straight at mine.

And I could tell in an instant that her act was a mirror of my own. It made me a little uneasy, for just a second. See, the other kids I knew in pictures seemed to struggle a lot to manage the public front we were all expected to put up: clever and witty, yet always polite. I could pull it off without much trouble. One look at Virginia, and I knew she could, too.

"The shooting schedule's been moved up a week," Maureen said. "You two will need to be here tomorrow for publicity stills. Filming starts a week from Monday."

"Why so soo—" I began, surprised, then caught myself. "Gosh." Too slow. Maureen had ordered me to never, never question her in public. I knew there'd be hell to pay. I tried to recover. "How unusual to have such a short break between pictures. I'll have to work hard on my lines next week."

A shadow crossed Virginia's face. Could she sense my fear?

"You both will," Maureen said, her expression not changing. "We'll have a line run-through today at the dance school. Three o'clock. Costume fittings and rehearsals next week. And if things work out, we'll have more for you two to do."

I grinned at her. It was the only way I could keep myself from groaning. She'd been wanting to work up a stage act for me and another kid, if only she could find the right kid. I could tell she was hoping Virginia was the one. Me, I wanted to stick to making pictures and let it go at that.

"Why, hello, Mr. Harkin," someone said a little extra loudly. Mr. Harkin, the head of the studio, was picking his way among the cables that snaked across the floor behind the cameras and lights. He didn't respond to the greeting.

Maureen pinched my shoulder and hissed, "Be on your toes."

I wasn't worried. Mr. Harkin liked me. I mean, not that we were great buddies or anything. But he'd given me a friendly smile now and then, and we'd had sort of a conversation once: I told him about how my parents had come over from England, and he told me his parents had come from Poland. He even wrote me a personal note after my last picture saying how much he enjoyed it. I liked to reread it whenever Maureen was being hard on me.

A chorus of "Hello-Mr.-Harkin"s rippled through the set. Without stopping, he raised a hand in acknowledgment, then bustled through the exit that led to the outdoor lot. Mr. Harkin kept a car and driver out there all the time.

Maureen relaxed. "Well, I have some business to attend to, Billy. Joe or someone can help you get cleaned up. Virginia, do you have a script?"

"Yes, Mrs. Fritz."

"Good. You'd better go. Your aunt looks anxious." She sent Virginia toward a mousy-looking woman who stood by the door. "Billy, I've got your copy of the script. I'll pick you up at two."

"I'll be ready, Mrs. Fritz!" I hoped that if I sounded extra enthusiastic she would forget that little slip earlier.

As it turned out, she did forget. But it wasn't because of my sparkling and dynamic performance, then or later at line rehearsal. It was because of what happened that day at a ritzy apartment in Coney Island. When we got back to Maureen's apartment in the evening, the phone rang and the voice on the other end gave Maureen the news that would change my life.

CHAPTER TWO

"What for?" Maureen said into the phone. Then: "Oh, my God."

I felt a flash of concern for her. I had a pretty good idea what the call was about, but it seemed to trouble her to the point where she had a genuine human reaction. I don't see this part of Maureen often, and it always touches me when I do. I can't help it. I do care about her. She's not much, but hey, when I'm in New York, she's the closest thing to a mom I've got.

Anyway, the instant of softness ended, as they always do, and Maureen's voice regained the businesslike hardness I was used to.

"How did he do it? . . . Yes, it is a good thing. I just hope this doesn't hurt us at the box office. . . . Billy? Well, they can't talk to him. What's Mr. Harkin saying? . . . Yes, of course. All right, I'll tell him. Thanks, Warren." She hung up.

I waited. Politely. I could feel the blood pounding in my ears.

"That was Warren Hill." Big surprise—the jerk and Maureen got along great. "Roscoe Muldoon's been arrested for murder. He killed Amelia St. Augustine in his apartment."

"That's impossible!" I blurted. "Roscoe wouldn't kill anyone. He's the nicest guy in pictures."

She looked at me sharply. "You watch what you say around other people, hear me? Roscoe's career is over, but I don't want this to wreck your career, too."

"I don't believe Roscoe did it." This was way too much back talk, but I didn't care. "He couldn't have."

"He could have, and he did. The police found him kneeling next to her body, in his apartment. Apparently he beat her up. Her head was cracked open." She took a deep breath and let it out. "Mr.

Harkin is sticking up for Roscoe, of course. Warren says reporters are swarming all over the studio, looking for everyone involved in *Call Me Pop*. I told him they couldn't talk to you, but he says they're obnoxious and crafty. So you'd better stay on your toes, just in case one of them finds you. If they do get to you, you tell them you hardly knew Roscoe, you don't know anything about him, and you didn't see him today. Got that?"

It gave me the creeps the way she talked about him as if he were dead. What I should have said at that point was: "Yes, Maureen." What I did say was: "Hardly knew him? That's baloney! Roscoe's my best friend in the whole world. If Mr. Harkin is sticking up for him, why can't I do it, too?"

Whap!

Maureen's slap burned my cheek. I staggered, lost my balance, and fell onto the couch.

"You'll do as I say!" Her voice was taking on a dangerous edge, and I knew I'd gone too far. She clenched her fists and breathed faster, then reached out toward the side table. I ran for my room. As I shoved the door closed, I heard the Manhattan phone book slam against it.

The next morning, the papers were full of Chubby Muldoon stories. Maureen tried to keep me from reading them, but I managed to sneak the *Post* into my room. I wanted to grab *Daily Variety*, too, but she wouldn't put it down.

"Comedian Jailed in Brutal Slaying of Actress," the headline informed me. I read on. "New York police arrested comic actor Roscoe 'Chubby' Muldoon yesterday after he was found kneeling next to the battered and lifeless body of actress Amelia St. Augustine, costar of Muldoon's upcoming film, *Call Me Pop*." Costar? Ha! Her part was minor. She played my mom, who abandons me in the second scene. But she's pretty well-known, so I guess they just assumed she was important in this one, too. Reporters. Don't they give a darn about facts?

"Miss St. Augustine apparently died from a deep wound to her head.

"The assault took place in Mr. Muldoon's apartment on Coney Island. A man who lives in the building heard a commotion overhead and called police to report shouting and fighting."

It went on about how Mr. Harkin was saying what a great guy Roscoe is, how there must be some mistake, blah blah blah.

Maureen had some errand or other to run, and she briefly considered taking me to school for the day. She had enrolled me in a private one, all nice and legal so no one could accuse her of contributing to my delinquency, but I never went while I was working on a movie. In the end, she decided to take me to the studio instead.

Well, you can imagine what the place was like when we arrived. Reporters and photographers everywhere, talking to anyone who wouldn't punch them out—and let me tell you, that narrowed the choices. These guys were climbing over pieces of scenery, dodging cameras, lights, and wind machines the stage crew was trying to get into place. You'd think someone could just throw the reporters out.

But no, there was Mr. Harkin, in the middle of the *Call Me Pop* set with a podium in front of him, and the reporters were gathering, notebooks in hand, and quieting down. Mr. Harkin told them how saddened he was by this tragedy, and that the studio would do whatever it could to comfort

Amelia's family at this difficult time. He said he knew it looked bad for Roscoe, but he had complete faith in Harkin Studios' number one star, and on like that. I was glad Roscoe had someone as powerful as Mr. Harkin on his side. So what if nobodies like Maureen pretended they didn't know him?

Maureen and I stood in the shadows while Mr. Harkin conducted his press conference. None of the newshounds had noticed me yet. Maureen's grip on my shoulder was like a vise, and it tightened when I tried to twist away.

Off to our left, some girls were talking. I had seen them around the studio. One was a tall, flaming redhead, and the other two were shorter and sort of blond—one brassy, the other bleachy white. They had the kind of show biz look that made you wonder if you'd recognize them if they washed their faces and let their hair grow out its real color. They called themselves actresses, but they were really chorus girls. Maureen turns up her nose at them, but my dad told me they deserve a lot of respect because they work so hard and get so little, and there are so many girls trying to get jobs and not many jobs to get. My dad always thinks dancers are special. He used to be one himself, when he was a kid.

"Why do you think he did it?" said the brassy blonde. My cheeks burned. Didn't anyone besides me believe Roscoe was innocent?

"Maybe he got tired of all her nagging," said the redhead.

"Yeah," the bleachy one said with an exaggerated fake hiccup. The three girls laughed.

"Hey, you girls." A cop walked over to the I'm-an-actresses.

I'd seen him around, too, mostly at studio parties. Mr. Harkin used him as a guard, to keep out riffraff, drunks, fans, and hangers-on. But in real life during the day, he was a New York cop in Flatbush, where the studio was. He was a big guy, probably taller than six feet, and he must have weighed three hundred pounds. On size alone, he could probably make any crook cower, but when you looked close you could see he was soft. He obviously paid plenty of attention to his appearance, though. Every time I saw him—including today—his sandy blond hair looked like it had just been cut, each hair precisely the right length and all slicked back. He wore those clunky cop shoes by day, but when he worked the studio parties he always had on shiny Italian loafers, like the ones Roscoe sometimes wore. And you should have seen this cop's fingernails! Filed and buffed and as perfect as any actress's. I guess he wanted his nails to look great because people were always eyeballing that knockout gold ring on his left pinkie.

So he walked up to the chorus girls, and they went into their act, tilting their heads, pushing their hips out to the side. Must be a habit. Give them an audience and this is what happens.

"I wanna ask you girls a few questions," the cop said.

"Why, Officer Mandell," Bleachy said, all coy and fakey, "what would you like to know?"

"Did any of you ever see Mr. Muldoon and Miss St. Augustine together?"

"They just finished a picture! Of course they were together." Hiccup. The three giggled. I wondered how much respect my dad would feel for dancers who could laugh so easily about a murder.

"I can see," Mandell said, sounding irritated, "that you girls are all broken up over Miss St.

Augustine's death. I'll try not to intrude upon your grief too much."

"Oh, Jimmy, come on," Flaming Red said. "Did you like her?"

He scowled. "Show some respect for the dead, will ya? Just tell me about the last time you saw Mr. Muldoon and Miss St. Augustine talking with each other."

"The usual," said Brassy. "She was going on about 'that demon rum' and how he should change his ways and stop drinking liquor. Chubby was so patient with her, so polite. But ya gotta figure he was tired of hearing it."

"Weren't we all," said Bleachy.

That was all I could catch of that interview, because Mr. Harkin had finished his press conference and the reporters had spotted me. I'm not sure whether she said it or it was my imagination, but I could hear Maureen's warning: Be on your toes.

The reporters reminded me of a school of fish, turning as one and gliding over to where we stood. Someone somewhere threw on a light, so I was no longer hidden in shadows. Movie people are quick when it comes to anything involving publicity.

Well-trained thespian that I am, I flung myself into the role of kid actor, the innocent in movieland, trying to understand this serious grown-up thing that had happened.

"I didn't— *don't* know Mr. Muldoon well," I said, then dared to add, "but I think he's really nice." I shot a look at Maureen to see if she'd heard. She had. I didn't care. I'd take the consequences for this.

No one was going to get me to desert Roscoe. No one.

CHAPTER THREE

The reporters must have had other scandals to chase. By two o'clock, they had all disappeared.

Maureen parked me with Mr. Goulding, the director, and left. It's kind of funny—the studio is where I work, sure, but it's also where I feel the most relaxed. When I'm with Maureen, she never lets me out of her sight. The guys at the studio are different. They trust me. They talk with me. Some of them ask me for directions to this or that place, because they all know that I know my way around the New York City subway system.

With the reporters gone, Mr. Goulding must have decided he didn't need to baby-sit me, so he turned me loose to hang around the set. I was surprised to see Virginia there, sitting in one of those chairs with the X-shaped legs and the canvas seat and back. She had her legs folded under her and was looking at a script in her lap. She wore overalls and a Yankees cap, and her hair hung down her back in two braids.

"Hello, Virginia." I walked over and displayed my public smile—I don't know why.

She looked up at me, glanced around quickly, then gave me a half-grin. I could see that my act was wasted on her. She saw through it. "Hi, Billy. I didn't know you were still around."

"I've been in Mr. Goulding's office. Maureen didn't want me saying anything honest—I mean *awkward*—to the reporters."

"No, we couldn't have that now, could we, Master O'Dwyer?"

"Why are you here today? Didn't anyone tell you the publicity stills have been put off until next week?"

"I took the call."

"Excuse me?"

"Mr. Goulding's secretary called, and I answered the phone. I just somehow forgot to pass the message along to Aunt Trudi, so she brought me in today. She won't mind when she finds out. It gives her an excuse to spend some more of my father's money shopping in the city."

We were silent for a moment. Then we both spoke at once.

"Billy—"

"Virginia—"

"I want to go see Roscoe," I said. "He's at the Tombs. It's only about a half-hour subway ride from here. Want to come with me?"

She slapped her script closed and jumped off the chair. "Sure. Do you know how to get to the jail?"

I puffed out my skinny chest.

"I know how to get everywhere."

She shot me that little half-grin again. Jeez, no point in trying to impress this girl. I hadn't meant to be a phony baloney, but I could see that's how I'd come across.

"Get out a lot, do you?" she asked.

"Well." I grinned—for real, this time. "Yeah.

Maureen doesn't know it, though. She thinks I just hang around here being polite and showing off my adorable freckles or something. So *please* don't say anything."

"You know what, Billy? I don't think Aunt Trudi would want me dashing off to any jailhouse, either." A perfect dramatic pause. "Let's go."

There are a lot of things you can't do when you're as famous as I am, like swear out loud or go to a regular school with regular kids. But one thing you can do is get in almost anywhere.

It happened that the watch officer at the Tombs was a big fan of Roscoe's silent pictures—especially the ones he'd made with Buster Keaton—and he'd also seen most of my pictures. Like ice cream dropped on the Coney Island boardwalk, he melted before my eyes. I gave him my autograph and signed autographs for his kids and wife and third cousin Elmore who lived in Dubuque. Then I introduced Virginia and told him she was going to be my costar in the *Rusty and Fred* series, and he wanted her to go through the whole procedure, too.

Finally, he took us to Roscoe's cell. Amazingly, it

looked just like the jail cells I'd seen in movies: small and square, with a cot in the back and bars in front. And just like a jailed movie character, Roscoe was sitting on the cot holding his head in his hands. It was eerie. I felt like I'd walked onto a set but someone had lost the script, so none of us knew where the story was going. As the watch officer let us into the cell, I saw Virginia shudder, looking around, and I knew she felt the unrealness of it, too.

"Hiya, Pardner." Roscoe straightened. I thought he was attempting a smile, but it was hard to tell. He didn't seem surprised to see me there.

I rushed to him and hugged him hard. "Hi, Roscoe," I said, pulling away. "How are you doing?"

"Pardner, I'm not doing very well at all." He stuck out a hand toward Virginia, an automatic gesture that seemed wildly out of place. "I'm Roscoe Muldoon."

She shook his hand. "Virginia Grady. It's nice to meet you, Mr. Muldoon."

Roscoe looked at me. "She's an actress, isn't she?" He'd pegged her instantly. The perfect politeness is a dead giveaway.

"Yup. She's Fred in the *Rusty and Fred* series."

"Ah. Well, nice to meet you, too, Virginia. Please call me Roscoe."

I couldn't take another minute of this baloney. "Roscoe, what happened?" I blurted.

He sagged, and I was instantly sorry I'd interrupted the small talk. I guess he needed people to treat him normally for a while. I felt like scum.

"I didn't do it, Pardner," Roscoe said. "I didn't kill her."

"I know that! It makes me so mad, the way everyone is saying—" Damn. I must have an open faucet where my mouth should be. I wished I could shut it off already.

"What are they saying?"

"Well, Mr. Harkin is sticking up for you and telling the reporters he believes in you and he's gonna do everything he can to bring the real killer to justice."

"Gosh, I didn't know he cared." His voice had an edge that didn't make sense to me. "What about the others?"

"Oh, you know. Stupid stuff. They're making up stories about why you did it. I mean, why they *think* you did it."

"Billy," Virginia cut in. "Why don't you quit before you depress Roscoe too much?" She sat on the cot beside Roscoe but got up quickly when it groaned with her weight. Roscoe's bulk must have been all it could handle. "What really happened, Roscoe? The paper said the police found you kneeling next to Miss St. Augustine's body."

"That much is true. I got home from—an errand."

"Your Wednesday pickup," I put in helpfully. Roscoe shot me a look. Somebody please just cut my tongue out of my head and save the world a lot of grief.

"Right," he said. "I put the box down outside the door and took out my key, but it was already unlocked. At first I thought someone had broken in, but there were no marks on the door or the knob. So I picked up my box and took it inside and set it down in the kitchen. I don't know how, but I walked right past her and didn't even see her there on the floor.

"I poured myself a drink. Boy, was that a mistake. And then I went back into the living room, and that's when I saw her. She was lying on the floor next to the coffee table. There was blood right around her head, and her arm was kind of twisted under her. Some of the blood got on the coffee table, too. God, I hate that table. I've banged my shins on it a thousand times."

I nodded. I'd done the same thing.

"I don't remember doing anything with my whiskey," Roscoe went on, "but I must have dropped the glass and spilled some on myself. I knelt down next to Amelia to see if she was conscious. But she was already gone. I was checking her neck for a pulse when the police got there."

"So they found you next to a dead body, smelling like alcohol, with an open bottle of bootleg whiskey on your kitchen table," Virginia summarized, sounding unsettlingly like a lawyer. Or a cop.

"Yes, that's exactly what happened. But I didn't do it."

"Did you see anyone else there?" she asked.

I held my breath.

"No, no one. Jimmy Mandell was the first cop to arrive."

"So you had been in the apartment what, maybe five minutes?" Virginia said.

"About that. Why?"

"How do you think the cops got there at just the right moment to find you like that?"

"Virginia, you've got me. I hadn't even thought of that. I guess I've been watching too many movies. It just seemed natural that the cops should show up right then." He shook his head. "I guess it's time for me to wake up to real life, isn't it?"

"Why did you act that way?" Virginia asked suddenly as we rode the subway back to the studio.

"I'm just a jerk," I said. "I have a big mouth. Okay?"

"No, that's not what I mean. I mean, why did you get so stiff when I asked Roscoe if he'd seen anyone else?"

Honest to spit, my mouth dropped open. I snapped it shut and stared at her. She stared right back. I made a decision. "I was there," I said.

"When Roscoe got to the apartment?" Miss Lawyer sounded surprised, which I kind of liked.

"No, I didn't see him. But I saw Amelia on the floor."

"You saw her?" Virginia's eyes were wide now.

"Well, not all of her. Just her feet. I didn't know then whose feet they were."

She waited, still staring at me. I took a deep breath.

"I went over yesterday to have lunch with Roscoe. Sometimes I do that. He takes me to Coney Island, and we eat hot dogs and ride the Steeplechase. I thought I'd surprise him, since we'd finished the retakes earlier than we'd expected."

"So you were the one who opened the door?"

"No, I was the one who closed it. It was open wide when I got there. I figured Roscoe had walked in with his hands full and hadn't come back to shut it. So I called out, 'Hey, Roscoe. It's me, Billy.' I think I took a step or two into the apartment before I saw Amelia." I shuddered, remembering. "Virginia, I didn't know what the heck was going on. I didn't know she was dead. But I knew something was wrong. I was scared there might be somebody hiding in the other room, and all I could think of was getting out of there as fast as I could. I was halfway back to the studio before it occurred to me that Roscoe might be in there and be hurt, too."

"Did you see the blood?"

"What a ghoul you are! No, I didn't see any blood. I told you, all I saw was her feet. I was in the doorway, and she was lying on the other side of the coffee table."

"But the paper made it sound like there was blood everywhere."

"There wasn't. Virginia, that apartment has white rugs. If there'd been blood splattered anywhere, I would have seen it."

"So why didn't you tell the police?"

I hesitated. "I didn't want to upset Maureen. And what good would it have done? I couldn't say for sure Roscoe wasn't there, since I didn't really go in."

"But you know things the police don't know." She was silent a minute. "You know what I think, Billy?"

I looked at her. I'd never met a kid like this one. "Yeah," I said. "I know exactly what you think. Because I think the same thing."

She stuck out her hand. "Partners?"

I shook it. "Partners. Who needs the cops? Roscoe's got us on his side."

CHAPTER FOUR

About five that afternoon, I sat at the studio guardhouse, waiting for Maureen to pick me up. The guard, Hal, is one of my chums. He was showing me a picture in a magazine of this great sailboat he wanted to have someday. He'd been reading all about these islands in the Caribbean and how they had pink beaches and you could sail on turquoise water from one island to another. I was about to ask him what his wife and five kids thought about this plan, when Lance Williams walked up.

"Hi, Lance," I said with my usual perky grin. I love it that I get to call all these big stars by their first names. Lance makes cowboy pictures, and he does all his own horse stunts. He tried to show me how to do some simple tricks once when I had a small part in a picture of his. I wasn't very good at it. This sounds goofy, but I wanted to get into pictures in the first place so I could have a pony all my own.

See, Maureen and her husband, Chester, had come to my dad's miniature golf course in Jamaica (the one in New York) to see me play. I was only nine and already had a reputation as a real hotshot on those little green fairways—not bragging or anything, but the *New York Post* even ran my photo in the sports pages. Well, Maureen took one look at my darling cowlick and perpetually pouting lower lip, decided I looked just like this comic strip character who was about to become a movie character, Skippy, and brought the strip's artist, Percy Crosby, out to meet me, too. I'd never heard of Skippy, or of Percy Crosby, at the time, but when they showed me the drawings of this kid, I could see why I had knocked them out.

They asked me if I wanted to be in the movies. I sized them up: Obviously they did not realize they were dealing with a nine-year-old and a sharp one at that. They wanted young, I gave them young. I opened my eyes wide.

"Could I have a pony, like Wesley Barry?" I asked. Wesley Barry is a kid who does cowboy pictures. His movies are pretty dumb, but I liked the idea of riding a horse like he did.

Maureen and Mr. Crosby laughed this "Oh-isn't-he-cute" laugh, and then Mr. Crosby said I could have a whole stable full.

One thing led to another. I took a screen test at Paramount. For some reason, the part went to Jackie Cooper and not to me. But that test was what launched my career, and what made it possible for me to stand around Harkin Studios shooting the breeze with guys like Lance Williams.

Lance ruffled my hair. "Hi, Billy," he said. "Pretty bad news about Roscoe, isn't it?"

"Yeah," I said. "I don't believe he did it, though. Do you?"

"I don't know what to believe, Billy. I've seen Roscoe lose his temper, and it was bad. It was at a party at his house in California. Have you been there?"

I shook my head, flattered that he'd even think I might have been hobnobbing with stars out in Hollywood. I'd never been west of Niagara Falls.

"Well, Roscoe had had a few drinks, and he actually picked up this little guy and threw him over a hedge and off his property! I never would have guessed he had the strength."

"Why did he do that?" I asked.

"I never found out. The two of them were having some kind of argument out in the yard."

"Was the little guy hurt?"

"No, no. He just got up and ran off, yelling some pretty choice words back over his shoulder. That part I did hear, because I'd come out to see what the fuss was about. But you know, other than that one time, I've never known Roscoe to be anything but a gentleman. He's not much in the looks department, but I want to tell you, I've seen women turn green with envy when they see the way he treats his wife."

"He's nice to everyone," I noted.

"Yes, you're right. Everyone. And a real straight-shooter. That's why we were willing to take a chance on his company."

"What company?"

"Catalina Productions." Lance stopped, probably wondering if he'd let out a secret he was supposed to keep. Then he snapped his fingers. "Didn't anyone tell you? Roscoe's contract with Harkin is about to expire, and he's been planning to start his own production company. He told me he wanted you to work with us, too. I just assumed you knew. I know he talked to that manager of yours—what's her name?"

"Maureen."

"Yes, Maureen. Billy, this could have been great. We had so much creative energy going into this."

"Wait, who is 'we'? Who else?"

"Well, me, and . . . I probably shouldn't name any of the others. This obviously isn't going to happen, with Roscoe out of the picture. He was the guiding force, and the rest of us were just looking for a lifeboat. I guess we're stuck with Harkin for the time being. I will tell you—" he looked around, then put an arm over my shoulders and leaned closer—"Roscoe was trying to get Buster Keaton to come on board. And it looked like he was gonna do it, too. Buster had a rough time at MGM, but he's a tremendous talent. You know, Roscoe and Buster are great friends." He stood back. "But as I said, it won't happen now."

I remembered something he'd said a minute ago. "But really, Lance, you don't think he killed her, do you?" I heard a note of desperation in my own voice. I wanted someone, some adult, to reassure me on this.

"You know, it's a funny coincidence that Amelia St. Augustine should die in that Coney Island apartment. That's where she lived when she was making *The Creature from the Grave*."

"She was staying with Roscoe?"

"No, no. It's the studio's place."

"The apartment in Coney Island?" I said.

"Yup. Harkin has that one and several smaller ones in Manhattan for his West Coast stars to live in when they're working here. The biggest names get to stay in Coney Island, of course. I hear Mr. Harkin stays there himself now and then, too. But keeping apartments is cheaper than putting his people up in hotels, and God knows Harkin's gotta watch every dime."

I realized he'd dodged my question again.

"Lance, come on. Do you think Roscoe killed Amelia?"

He sighed and ruffled my hair a second time. People do that to me a lot.

"What I think is that what I believe and what you believe is not going to matter a whit. And you know the worst part? What really, truly happened isn't going to matter a whit. All that matters is what people *think* happened. Believing is seeing, Billy." He gave me a manly pat on the back. "See you around, kid."

I knew I had to pick my words carefully that night.

Chester was working a night shift at the hospital, so it was just me and Maureen at home. I scurried around the apartment trying to do anything I could think of to put her in a good mood. I volunteered to bring up the mail. I washed the dishes. I sat down with my script and studied without being reminded. I even offered to put her favorite record on to play. That was when she finally smiled.

"That would be nice," she said, "but turn it down low so I can read the paper." Maureen had her usual evening glass of gin on the table beside her. Like everyone else in the movie business, she had her system for getting around Prohibition. I never knew where it came from, but Maureen had her gin delivered right outside our door in white milk bottles, once a week. The gin's effect on her was unpredictable. Sometimes she'd go into one of her rages over the stupidest little thing; other times, she'd talk with me about studio gossip or her plans for my career. And some nights, like tonight, she would sit quietly and read all evening.

I put on the record as she'd instructed. After I got the volume just right, I turned to her ever so casually, hoping she didn't hear me gulp. "Maureen," I began. My palms were clammy. Good thing they didn't start sweating until after I'd gotten my mitts off her precious record. "Maureen, I was talking to Lance Williams today while I was waiting for you."

"Oh?" She didn't look up. So far, so good.

"And he said Roscoe was planning to start his own production company. Lance said he and some other people were going to go with Roscoe."

"Mm-hmm."

"And he said he thought I'd already know this

because Roscoe had talked to you about me working for his new company too." I held my breath.

Maureen looked at me over the top of her reading glasses. "He did talk to me," she said at last. "We couldn't break your contract, of course, but you'd be free in six months, after the *Rusty and Fred* series is done. Assuming things can go on that long." She pulled off the glasses and rubbed her eyes, then looked up at me again. "I'm sorry, Billy. It would have been a wonderful opportunity for us. Roscoe had some very good ideas for pictures you could be in. He thought the world of you."

Maureen went back to her reading. It didn't even seem to have occurred to her that I'd dared to question something she'd done—or not done, in this case.

And me, I was reeling. Not at what she'd said about Roscoe, or his plans. My head swam because in the two years I'd lived with her, in all the times she had thrown pots and pans and phone books at me, or twisted my wrists, or shoved me against the wall, I'd never heard her say those three words: "I'm sorry, Billy."

CHAPTER FIVE

The next day was Friday, and Maureen put me on the train to Providence. She always unloaded me for the weekends because she and Chester liked to go out to nightclubs and have card parties with their friends. Most of the time I stayed with my Uncle Bob, who lived in Queens, pretty close to the studio, but this time she wanted me out of the city and away from all the fuss, so she sent me home to my parents in New Bedford.

Maureen didn't like my parents much. She was always saying my mom was an idiot and my dad didn't know what was best for me. She even tried to get him to sign me over and make her my legal guardian. Fat chance! I hated to hear her running them down, but I had learned to ignore it. Arguing with her was out of the question. But nothing she could say or do was going to turn me against my parents.

See, my dad's the greatest. He's the one I got my performing talent from, and he's tickled to have me in movies. He used to be in vaudeville himself, and I think he would have stayed in show business if he hadn't gotten married. He loves it all, just like I do. The lights, the music, the audiences, the rush you get right before a performance when something inside you says, "I can't remember a thing I'm supposed to do out there," and you go out and knock 'em dead, anyway.

My mom, on the other hand, doesn't see the appeal of any of it. When Maureen first told my parents I would need to live with her in New York, my mom refused. She told Maureen she'd rather have me stay home, get through high school, and go to work in the mill like a normal kid. She and my dad had a big fight over it—actually, several fights. But my dad got his brother, my Uncle Bob, to promise he'd keep an eye on me, so my mom gave in. She still cries every time she and my dad put me on the train back to New York.

Anyway, my dad picked me up in Providence that Friday night and drove me back home to Massachusetts, and we all spent the evening playing whist. Our fourth was my Auntie Annie, whose house my parents and my sister, Olive, lived in. Olive, being only three, didn't play cards yet.

The next morning, I helped my dad bottle some of his homemade beer. I know what you're thinking, but it wasn't like that. He had a permit to make that beer. He'd been gassed in the war, and a doctor wrote him a prescription or something that made it okay for him to brew beer for himself even though making beer was illegal because of Prohibition. He was supposed to inhale the fumes from all the malt and then drink one bottle every night. It must have worked: He seemed pretty healthy to me.

And since he had all that brewing and bottling equipment, and especially since he'd been laid off at the mill six months earlier and we needed the money, he'd started filling a few extra bottles and selling them to some of the guys from his club. My dad's not a crook; he says it's just hard times and you do what you have to do to feed your family. Which is why we spent that Saturday morning filling bottles over a tub in the basement and packing up the ones he'd done the week before so we could deliver them.

Of course, he'd read all about Roscoe. "It's a dirty business, that," he said. "I can't think what made him do it."

"He didn't do it, Dad," I said. I capped a bottle and moved another under the keg for filling. "Roscoe would never hurt anyone."

"Oh, I know you like him." He ruffled my hair—even my own father! "But the papers said the cops found him kneeling over her body, blood everywhere. Now how could that be if he hadn't just beat her up?"

"The papers are wrong," I said, unsure whether I should correct him on the matter of the blood. My palms suddenly felt clammy as the full horror of Amelia's death swept over me. Those feet I had seen, so still, in the silence of Roscoe's apartment. The feet of someone I'd worked with and talked with only a day earlier. Dead. Murdered. Lying not five yards away from me.

The bottle slipped from my hands and shattered in the tub.

"Here now," my dad said, "be careful with them bottles. Did you hurt yourself?" He took my hands and examined them for cuts.

"No," I said. "Sorry, Dad."

"That's all right. We've got more. We'll clean this up when we finish filling." He handed me another clean, empty bottle. I held it under the keg, pushing the picture of Amelia from my mind.

"I'll give you this," he said. "It doesn't seem like something a man with his talent would do. He's a big star. Why should he wreck his career like that?"

"Dad, he didn't kill her. He told me so himself."

He looked at me for a moment. I could tell he'd instantly figured out how I'd gotten Roscoe's version of the story. "Did Maureen take you to the Tombs?"

"No. She thinks I stay at the studio when she leaves me there."

"Billy, I know you think it's fun running around on them subways, but New York is not New Bedford."

This discussion was going nowhere I wanted it

to go. "So," I said brightly, determined to return to the Roscoe matter at some better time. "What's new with you, Dad? Any new job leads?"

"Nah, nothing yet. But I did pretty well at the races this week. Come out ten dollars to the good." He pulled something from his pocket. "Look here. This one was supposed to be a sure thing. Was it buggery! I'd have been fifteen dollars ahead if I hadn't bet on this nag. It's been a bad year for favorites. I should have stuck with my long shots."

We're big on horse racing. My cousin is a jockey in Canada, and that's kind of made the whole family into regular readers of the *Daily Racing Form*.

"That's great, Dad. Ten dollars. Is that enough for you and Mom to move back to Query Street?"

"Not yet. But we're getting there."

When my dad lost his job, they sold their furniture and moved in with Auntie Annie. This all happened while I was away in New York. I'd thought my pay was pretty good, but somehow it wasn't keeping my parents in the home they'd rented for years.

"The mill's just barely hanging on," Dad said. "Good thing for us your mum still has her job. I see hard times are even hitting the studios. The trades say Harkin's not paying his bills and the studio'll go under if it doesn't put out something what'll make some big money."

"Mr. Harkin's smart, Dad. He won't let the studio go broke." I'd heard rumors of trouble, but they didn't mean much to me. I had a contract, and the studio had to pay me—that's all I really knew. Which is not to say much of the money ever crossed *my* sweaty little palms.

"It's like this all over the country!" he went on. "Hoover, what does he know? Keeping all the government money like it was his own, when he should be spending it to put people back to work. I'll tell you, there's got to be a better way than just pushing people off into poorhouses when they lose their jobs. Lucky we had our Annie to take us in."

He went on like that, about President Hoover and the Depression, while we finished bottling the beer for his pals. And he kept on about it as we drove across town to deliver the stuff. Once my dad gets going on a subject, it's hard to stop him. I knew I'd have to wait a long time to bring up Roscoe again.

Our first stop was in a Portuguese neighborhood. I loved coming to this block because of the smells. Some of the Portuguese families raised chickens and rabbits in their backyards, along with vegetables. Mixed in with the odors of live animals was the scent of the spicy *linguiça* that always seemed to be cooking. My parents never socialized at the homes of Portuguese families, but I had a few times before I went into pictures. One of my best chums at school had been a Portuguese kid named Leon. Actually, Leon's American; his parents are from the Old Country. At school, they always taught us that even though our parents stayed among people from their own country, we kids were all Americans and should all live together.

Dad left me outside on the porch steps while he took his beer into the Silvas' house. It was about a block from Leon's house, so I wasn't surprised when he and his little brother came tearing down the street on their bicycles. "Leon," I yelled.

He looked over and waved, then circled back and stopped in front of me. "Hey, Mr. Movie Star!"

"Aw, Leon." The only time I wish I weren't in pictures is when I'm around my old pals in New Bedford. "That's a swell bike. Can I try it?"

Leon hopped back on the bike and took off, riding in circles in the street.

"Leon, come on," I called. "Please?"

"Ooh," he said, circling past me. "Mr. Movie Star wants to ride my bike! Will you autograph the tires?"

I had no idea why he was being such a jerk, but it made me angry. I got up off the steps and walked into the street in time to catch him on his next loop. I grabbed the handlebars and stopped the bike. Leon nearly fell off. "Hey," he said, "let go."

"Why won't you let me ride your bike?" I gripped the handlebars harder to try to stop the trembling in my voice. "Huh, Leon? Why not?"

"Let go of my bike, Billy," he said. "You can't take whatever you want just because you're a big movie star." He jerked the bike from my hands and stuck his tongue out at me.

I could feel my right hand balling into a fist.

"Billy!" My dad was at the Silvas' door. "Here now, what's going on?" He charged down the steps and out to the street. He stood on my right and put an arm firmly across my shoulders, which made it impossible for me to throw a punch.

EILEEN HEYES

"He tried to take my bike," Leon said. "He tried to knock me off and steal it."

"Is that true, Billy?"

"I just wanted to try it," I muttered, looking at some fascinating stones in the street. I pushed them around with my shoe.

Dad made me apologize to Leon, and we left. He didn't say any more about the bike incident that day, and neither did I.

That night I dreamed I was being chased by something I couldn't see. Leon's bike appeared, and I ran to get on it so I could escape. But every time I got near it, it rolled away. I ran and ran, reaching for that bike. But it was always out of my reach, like it was refusing to save me.

I woke up with tears running down my cheeks.

CHAPTER SIX

Monday morning at six, the whole *Rusty
and Fred* gang was in the makeup room. It
was really more like a closet. Even though
we were just going to shoot publicity stills
that day, we had to put on all the same
makeup as if we were filming.

There were me and Virginia, of course,
and Bobby Jordan, Sam Gray, Anthony
Seelye, and the Jackson brothers—
Hamilton and Jefferson. The Jacksons were
the only Negro kids in the gang. Then there
was Denny Carlisle, who played the namby-
pamby kid that our gang would always be
picking on. I'd worked with him and Ham

Jackson before, and we'd had a ball together, but the others were new to me.

The studio was pretty much back to normal. Mr. Harkin, having said his bit for the reporters, had barred them from the property. They'd apparently gotten the message—or lost interest—because there hadn't been any reporters hanging around the front gate when Maureen and I arrived. I could tell she was relieved. And hey, when she's relieved, *I'm* relieved. She was so relieved, in fact, that she checked me in with Warren Hill and left almost immediately. I like to see Maureen feeling secure.

When we got out of makeup, the photographer still hadn't arrived. We had to put on our costumes, but that would only take a couple minutes. This is the way it is in pictures: You always have to get up at four so you can start getting made up at six so you can be ready to work by seven but wait around till eight-thirty or so before the crew is ready.

Ham started humming to himself and doing a little time step on the concrete floor of the sound-stage. Before long, his humming got louder, his body swayed with the rhythm he was tapping out, and I could see he'd left the rest of us behind. Ham's a year older than me, and he's a great tap dancer. Even better than my dad. The other kids gathered around and clapped the beat for him. Ham looked a little surprised, then grinned. I went up beside him and tried to match some of his steps, and he slowed down and did some simpler moves so I could keep up.

Then he said, "Hey—challenge!" He shuffled off to Buffalo for a few bars. I loved a tap challenge, even though I knew Ham could dance rings around me. I matched him step for step when he gave me the floor. He made it tougher for me with the next step, a single wing and jump, but I managed to match that, too.

"Hey, Billy," he said, sounding impressed. "You've been practicing." In my wildest dreams, I was tap dancing like Ham Jackson, to the tumultuous cheers of an astonished audience. My dad would burst with pride.

Then Ham got me. He did a double wing with that perfect rolling motion that made it look like he could fly if he wanted to and finished with a split. I gave it my best shot, but fell on my butt. We were both laughing as Ham reached down to help me up.

The next thing that happened surprised me.

EILEEN HEYES

Virginia stepped out of the group and matched all of Ham's steps, right through the double wing and split, which she could do because she was wearing these baggy pants. I hadn't expected her to be so good. The guys all clapped for her. She sprang to her feet and took a bow, then held out a hand toward me and Ham, signaling our little audience to applaud us, too, which they did. Then the others headed off toward wardrobe.

"Billy," she said when they'd gone. "We need to talk about our investigation."

"Our investigation's over. Didn't you see the *Post* today?"

"No. Why?"

"It sounds like the cops are about to let Roscoe go. The district attorney can't figure out any reason Roscoe would want to kill Amelia. No motive, no case." I brushed my hands together. As far as I was concerned, the whole thing was wrapped up.

She rolled her eyes. "I notice he's still in jail, Sherlock. I think we ought to keep going. Even if Roscoe's off the hook, we can still find the killer." Her eyes gleamed in a way that unnerved me. Suddenly I realized Virginia wasn't in this to save

Roscoe. She was enjoying her role as a detective.

"So," she said, "let's start at the beginning. What do we know so far?"

I knew I should at least make an effort to get her off this kick, but the drama of the chase was more than I could resist. I thought hard. "Not much," I said. I told her about my conversation with Lance Williams.

"Did he say anything about Amelia?"

"No. Just that it was bad news about Roscoe."

"Did you ask him about her?"

I could feel my cheeks burn under the thick makeup. "I didn't think of it. I mean, what would he know?"

"Billy, you goof! Don't you see? We have to find out everything about her before we can hope to figure out why someone would want to kill her. You must know some things about her. What was she like?"

"Boring," I said. "Nobody liked her because she was always trying to talk them out of drinking liquor. She thought Prohibition was the greatest idea since talking pictures."

"Hm, so plenty of people were annoyed with

her. That's not much of a reason to kill someone. Did she have any friends?"

I thought again. "Rachel, in wardrobe. She's the only one Amelia ever laughed with, as far as I could see."

Virginia looked satisfied. "Well, then, we'll just have to talk to Rachel, won't we?"

"Why? Rachel didn't kill her. She's the only one who liked her."

Virginia rolled her eyes again. I hate it when she does that.

We waited outside wardrobe until the other guys had finished getting dressed.

"Hiya, Rachel," I said, walking in. "Have you met Virginia Grady?"

"Hiya, Billy." She stuck a hand out to Virginia. "Pleased to meet you." She pronounced it "pleezta meecha." I liked the way Rachel talked. Pure Brooklyn, straight off the street, nothing phony about her. She obviously hadn't tried to unlearn her accent the way I'd had to unlearn mine. She was one of the few people I'd met at the studio who didn't want to act.

Rachel consulted her costume list and turned to the rack where she'd organized the *Rusty and Fred* wardrobe, then handed each of us a hanger full of clothes. My costume wasn't all that different from my regular clothes; Virginia was supposed to wear some scruffy dungarees, a man's shirt, and the Yankees cap she'd had on the week before. Tomboy stuff.

"It's so sad, what happened to Amelia St. Augustine," Virginia said. I could have smacked her. Hadn't she ever heard of subtlety?

Rachel's shoulders sagged. "Yeah," she said. "Really sad. She was a gem." She sniffed, then dabbed her nose with her sleeve.

"You were pretty good friends with her?" Virginia asked, her voice full of understanding.

"Yeah," Rachel said again. "I think I was the only friend she had around here."

"Why didn't she have more friends?"

I swear that girl will grow up to be a cop.

Rachel looked at Virginia, then at me, and choked out a sad little laugh. "Billy can probably tell you all about it—right, Billy? Amelia didn't get snockered with the rest of them. That's what they didn't like."

"She didn't want anyone to drink," I put in, ever helpful.

"Nah," Rachel said. "She didn't. She hated booze because of what it did to her pop."

"What's that?" Virginia asked.

"Killed him. He was bad news, anyway, with all his boozing and gambling and running around on her mom. She told me it was almost a relief for all of them when he finally drank himself to death. But you know, no one really wants to see their pop die."

I imagined my own dad dying and felt a lump rise in my throat. I couldn't think of anything that would hurt more. "Gosh," I said, "I didn't know that about her dad. No wonder she acted that way."

"But was that a reason for him to kill her?" Rachel asked, bursting into sobs. For a second I didn't catch her meaning.

"We don't think Roscoe killed her, Rachel," Virginia said soothingly.

"No?" Rachel's puffy red eyes drilled a look into Virginia. "Then you tell me why he was kneeling over her body in his own apartment when they found her. What was she doing there, if he didn't lure her there to knock her off? Everyone wanted to shut her up, so he went and did it."

Rachel collapsed into the one rickety chair in wardrobe and held her face in her hands, sobs still shaking her. Virginia put a hand on Rachel's shoulder. Finally Rachel looked up. "You kids better get dressed and get back to the set," she said. "Go on, I'll be all right."

"Are you sure?" Virginia the saint again.

"Yeah." She smiled a little. "Thanks, kid. I guess I needed a little cry. Go on, now."

We picked our way back through the forest of light stands and sections of scenery toward the *Rusty and Fred* set.

"She's got a good point," Virginia said.

"Which one's that?"

"Why was Amelia at Roscoe's apartment?"

I stopped. I'd never thought to question that. "Well," I said. "I guess there's only one way to find out, isn't there, partner?"

CHAPTER SEVEN

"So this is where Harkin Studios puts its big stars." Virginia leaned her head back to look up at the Coney Island apartment building. It was a pretty impressive place from the outside, and even better from the inside.

I led her into the lobby, and she cranked her head back again, taking in all the gold curly things in the ceiling, which was really high, and the big brass chandelier. The floor was shiny black marble; that was my favorite part. Our steps echoed as we walked over to the little elevator, where a pimply kid in a uniform waited for passengers. People who could afford to live in a place like this did not walk up stairs.

We shouldn't have been surprised—but we were—to find the door of Roscoe's apartment locked. Virginia looked at me expectantly. "Well?" she said.

"Well what?"

"Well, open it. Don't you have a key?"

"Why would I have a key?"

She did that thing with her eyes again, only this time her whole head rolled, too. "You mean to tell me we came all the way out here with no way to get into this apartment?"

I started to puff my chest and say something arrogant, but then I remembered the last time I'd tried that on her. I went for humble instead. "Let's talk to the building super," I said.

"Great idea. I'll bet he'll be delighted to let two kids into an apartment where there's been a murder. Especially when we tell him we're investigating the crime. Yup, I can see that happening."

"All right," I said, losing patience. "Then you let me handle it. I'll get us in."

"Be my guest."

I remembered something I'd read in the *Post*. "Listen, Virginia. Why don't you snoop around and talk to some of the neighbors. The paper said some guy on the floor below was the one who called the cops. It said he heard shouting and fighting upstairs. See if you can find him, and see what he heard. Whoever that guy is, he might be the closest thing we'll get to an actual witness."

Her eyebrows went up. "I read that!" she said. "But I'd forgotten. Billy, you're a genius."

She headed toward the stairwell, and I took the elevator down to find the super.

I'd met him once, back when Roscoe and I first started making our Coney Island expeditions. Short, husky guy, with dark curly hair and soft white skin. He had these bushy eyebrows that made him look kind of scary to me, but Roscoe had said the guy was a huge movie fan. Maybe that's why he was so pale: too much time in the dark.

When he opened his office door, he looked down at me over these glasses with half-lenses. He took them off and folded them up. "Yeah?" he said.

I felt certain he'd have greeted an adult with something more along the lines of "Can I help you?" which annoyed me. But I kept a humble face. Humble, innocent, perky, and serious, all at the same time.

"Hello. I'm Billy O'Dwyer." I waited for this to have its effect, but his face didn't change. "I'm a friend of Roscoe Muldoon's." I thought fast. "The studio sent me over to pick up some of his things."

"You know Chubby Muldoon?" He softened a little. I started to correct him, but realized that the public knew Roscoe as Chubby, and this guy didn't use the nickname disrespectfully. Then I could see the light come on. "Hey, you're the one from *Ain't That Swell,* aren't you? Um, Billy, um . . ."

"O'Dwyer," I finished for him. "That's right. Have you seen the movie?"

"Sure." He grinned. "Seen it five times. Damn! I don't know why I didn't recognize you right off. Gosh, I'm sorry. Come on in."

I followed him into the office, itching to get on with my investigation.

"Here, I have this book," he said, rummaging in a drawer. I spotted the rack of apartment keys on the far wall. The hook below Roscoe's apartment number, 707, was empty. "Here it is. Could I have your autograph, Billy? Just write it 'To Alvin.'"

"Sure." I grinned at him, hoping he wouldn't notice me gritting my teeth. While I wrote something about good wishes, I said, "So, Alvin, can you let me into Roscoe's place? I know exactly what Mr. Harkin wants me to pick up."

"Oh, he forget something?"

"Uh, yeah," I said. "Yeah, he forgot a few things. He gave me a list." Please, I thought, don't ask to see it.

Alvin reached toward the key rack, then saw the empty hook and frowned. "Hm," he said. "Well, I'll let you in with mine. Come on. Gosh, I loved *Ain't That Swell*." He went on about his favorite parts, and how funny the scene with the puppies was, and on and on. I'm used to this, so I took it all in politely. I was glad he didn't see anything odd in the studio sending a star instead of some flunky to fetch stuff from the apartment.

I hoped he'd leave me alone once he let me into Roscoe's apartment, but no such luck. He stood in the doorway while I tried to act as if there were something in particular I'd come for.

It had only been five days since Amelia's death,

and the apartment was eerily like I remembered it. To my right was the closed kitchen door; in front of me and to the left was the living room. Nothing seemed to have been moved, not even the table with the shin-bashing edges. I walked around it to see where the body had been. A brown crust covered a roundish spot about nine inches across on the carpet, a foot or so out from the coffee table. Dried blood from Amelia's head. A few smaller crusty spots lay between the big puddle and the table. And was that a smudge on the table, too?

My stomach churned. I don't know why, but I'd thought all traces of the violence would be cleaned up. Then it hit me: one small pool of blood. The papers had had it wrong. I felt a grim satisfaction at having been right about this. But the question remained: So what?

I retraced Roscoe's footsteps as he'd described them. Front door to kitchen (where there was no case of bootleg now). Kitchen back to living room. Yes, I could see how he could walk in carrying a box and not catch sight of a body on the living room floor. At the edge of the white rug, I looked down. A light brown stain spread out at my feet.

The whiskey Roscoe had dropped.

Yes, yes. It was true. It had happened exactly the way he'd said it had. I let my chin fall to my chest and my shoulders sag, feeling weak with relief. I hadn't realized until that moment that I'd doubted him.

"Billy, you okay?" Alvin asked.

"What? Oh, sure. Sure, I'm fine. I'm just, um, trying to remember where Mr. Harkin said those things were." I looked around. "That closet in the entryway. That's where he said to look. Now I remember." I hoped there would be something in the closet I could grab to make this ploy look convincing. I marched over and tried the knob. It was locked.

"Well?" Alvin said.

"Well what?"

"Don't you have the key?"

I could have sworn I'd had this conversation already. "No," I said. "Mr. Harkin said it would be unlocked. Oh, well. Just open it with yours."

"Can't." Alvin shrugged. "All I got's the master for the front doors. Any locks on inside doors, the residents have put in. Mr. Muldoon would have that key, unless the cops took it away from him."

"Oh, sure," I said. "Mr. Harkin must not have known that Roscoe put a locking knob on this door. We'll have to get the key from Roscoe."

Out of ideas and unable to wangle any time alone in the apartment, I decided to give up for the day. "Well, I guess this was just a wasted trip. Thanks for your help, Alvin."

"Pleasure," Alvin said. "And thank you for the autograph. I can't wait to tell my mom. She loves your pictures, too."

I managed what I thought was a chipper grin. Maureen makes me practice my grins in front of a mirror, so I can pretty much tell what they look like.

Alvin and I rode down in the elevator and said our good-byes, and I clopped across the big lobby and out into the sunshine.

Virginia rushed up to me. "Billy," she said with a thoroughly convincing breathlessness. "Something strange is going on."

"Did you find the guy who called the cops?"

"There isn't one."

"Isn't one what?"

"Guy."

"You mean no one was home?"

"I mean I talked to some of the neighbors on the sixth floor, and some on the fifth. The apartment right under Roscoe's has been vacant for two months, and you can't hear any noise from the seventh floor when you're on the fifth floor."

"So you're saying someone in another apartment on the sixth floor made the call?"

"No, no one on the sixth floor called."

"How can you be so sure?"

"Because there are no men on that floor at all. All the tenants are women."

CHAPTER EIGHT

The next morning, the papers were full of the Chubby case again. Mr. Harkin had held another press conference Monday afternoon while Virginia and I were in Coney Island. I almost laughed out loud when I read the story he'd given the reporters:

"Studio owner Joseph M. Harkin said the brutal slaying of Amelia St. Augustine had obviously been the work of a lunatic. Mr. Harkin said that Miss St. Augustine had gone to the apartment of Roscoe 'Chubby' Muldoon to join Mr. Muldoon for lunch on that fateful Wednesday, never imagining that before the day was over her blood would be splashed all over Muldoon's luxurious furniture."

I groaned. The part about the splashing blood must have come from the reporter's imagination, not Mr. Harkin's mouth. Besides, the luxurious furniture probably belonged to Mr. Harkin, not Roscoe. I read on.

"'They were the best of friends,' Mr. Harkin said. 'Roscoe admired Amelia very much. I often heard him asking her out for lunch or dinner.'"

Something about this part made me uneasy, but I wasn't sure why. Other than the fact that it was a lie, I mean.

"Mr. Harkin said that Miss St. Augustine must have arrived at Mr. Muldoon's apartment before Mr. Muldoon did, and she must have been followed by a murderous lunatic. The crazed pursuer, Mr. Harkin theorized, savagely beat the actress and left her in a pool of blood, then fled. Shortly thereafter, Mr. Harkin said, Mr. Muldoon arrived and found the already lifeless body." Then the paper repeated the stuff from the cops about the downstairs neighbor calling and all.

I had to hand it to Mr. Harkin. Everything he'd told the reporters was baloney, and I was sure he knew it. Roscoe was courteous to Amelia, but I had never seen them have an actual conversation. She was always cold to him, when she wasn't on one of her rants about alcohol. They worked together and kept their distance. But Mr. Harkin was standing up for Roscoe, doing his best to clear his name.

Maureen dropped me off at the studio around ten. Virginia was already there, curled up again in the canvas chair and this time reading the paper.

"If we can figure out the answer to this, we can crack the case." First words out of her mouth.

"Hello, Billy," I said. "Hello, Virginia," I replied. She just looked at me. I could tell she wanted to roll those eyes and was willing herself not to. It was kind of sweet, I thought. "Virginia, we went over this yesterday. Just because the tenants are all women doesn't mean—"

"You didn't meet these women, Billy. They were not the type to have men in their apartments in the middle of the day."

"As if you would know?"

She lifted her chin in a haughty way that reminded me of, well, myself. "A woman can tell these things about another woman."

"Oh yes, of course. Now if only we knew a woman we could ask."

She swatted me with the newspaper. "Smart aleck," she muttered. "I think someone other than a neighbor called the police. Maybe the real killer. Maybe the real killer was trying to get Roscoe caught with the body."

"Oh, come on. Don't you think that's a little far-fetched?"

"No, I don't." She looked past me. "Go ask *him*."

I turned and saw Jimmy Mandell, notebook in hand, talking with one of the lighting guys. The guy was shaking his head and saying something. Jimmy closed the notebook and turned toward the door.

"Jimmy," I called. I trotted over to catch him.

"Yeah?"

"Hiya, Jimmy. How's the investigation coming?" I was a little miffed that he should take such a cool tone with me, but I tried to sound friendly. "Have you found any good leads?"

"Leads? Now why would I need to look for leads? The guy we want is safely behind bars."

"Um, I just thought, you know, you were asking questions and taking notes, so I thought—"

"Gathering evidence. We still gotta prove the case."

"But the paper said the D.A. can't show a motive."

"That don't matter. Everyone knows who done it."

"Aw, Jimmy, you've got it all wrong. Roscoe didn't kill anyone. He'd never do a thing like that. You know him well enough to know that, don't you?"

"I don't know nothing like that. What I know is that some guy called me to report a very loud argument right over his head in Muldoon's apartment. What I know is that Amelia St. Augustine is dead. And what else I know is that I found him there myself, with his hands around her throat. I know he killed her. That's what I know."

"So who was this guy who called you?"

"He wouldn't gimme his name. Had an accent. Like Russian, or Hungarian, one of those." He brushed a strand of sandy blond hair from his forehead, that socko ring of his catching the light from one of the spots overhead.

"Nice ring," I said, stalling while I tried to think what else I should ask him about.

"You like that?" He seemed pleased.

"Sure, it's swell. Almost looks like real gold."

"It *is* real," he said. "Genuine eighteen-carat gold." He held it up and moved his pinkie to admire its flashing reflections.

"The closet," I blurted, suddenly remembering.

"Huh?"

"The closet in the entryway of Roscoe's apartment. Did you look in there for evidence?"

"Yeah. Just to be thorough. Nothing in there belongs to Muldoon, though."

"How'd you get it open?"

"Mr. Harkin gave me the—and how might you know it would be tough to open?"

I felt the blood rush to my cheeks and for once wished Virginia were at my side to cover me in her skillful, lawyerlike way. "Oh, Virginia and I were just taking a look around," I said, trying to sound casual. "And we couldn't help noticing that the closet was locked. The building super said—"

"When was this?"

"Yesterday. But the building super—"

"Listen to me, kid. That's a murder scene, see? It's no place for a couple of kids to go snooping around.

What were you doing, playing detective?"

My face felt like it was on fire.

"So you think you're gonna find something to get your pal Chubby off the hook? I got news for you. Butt out. You hear what I'm saying? You don't know what you're fooling around with here."

"But if there's evidence in the closet—"

"There ain't no evidence in that closet. Nothing but a bunch of stuff Mr. Harkin doesn't have any better place to store."

"Like what?"

"Like none of your business, that's what."

I hadn't really expected an answer, but it was worth a try.

"You two just keep your noses away from that apartment and out of this investigation. Hear what I'm saying?"

Jimmy stuck his notepad and pencil in his pocket, turned, and clumped out.

At last, Virginia appeared at my shoulder. "Well?" she said.

"Jeez, don't sneak up on me like that."

"Well, what did you learn?"

I liked the way she put that. Not what did he

say, but what did I learn? It made me feel like Sherlock Holmes, reading all those clues in what people didn't say and didn't do, as much as in what they did say and do. "I learned that he really doesn't want us investigating this case."

"What a surprise."

"And everything in the closet belongs to Mr. Harkin. He gave Jimmy the key and let him look around inside, and Jimmy didn't find anything connected with the case, so he just left it all there."

"And?"

"And what?"

"And where's the key now?"

"I don't know. Jimmy probably gave it back to Mr. Harkin. Why?"

"Because we still need to see what's in there."

"Nothing's in there. Aren't you listening to me? Just some stuff of Mr. Harkin's."

"Billy, listen. Jimmy Mandell thinks Roscoe is the killer. He might have overlooked something that would give us a clue. Maybe the real killer dropped something and it slipped under that closet door."

"Don't take this personally, Virginia, but your theories really stink."

"What did he say about the call?"

"It was a guy with an accent. The guy said there was shouting and fighting right over his head."

"And we know that's not true, don't we?"

"So what do we do now?"

"Easy, Watson. We've got to see what's in that closet."

Fifteen minutes later, I was talking to Alice, Mr. Harkin's secretary. We agreed how good it was that Mr. Harkin was spending the day on Long Island, that he sure needed the break. We both shook our heads and lamented about Roscoe. We said how excited we were about the *Rusty and Fred* series starting up, and how we thought it would turn things around for kid-gang pictures, which hadn't been doing well lately.

Suddenly Virginia rushed in, out of breath. "Alice," she gasped, "you've got to come quick. There's a man outside trying to sneak in through the dressing room window. I think he's a reporter."

"What can *I* do?" Alice said. "Did you call the security guard?"

"I can't find him," Virginia said. "Please, no one else is around. You've got to come."

"All right, all right." She followed the frantic Virginia out, nearly stumbling in her spike heels.

I closed the outer door behind them and dashed into Mr. Harkin's office. I pulled his desk drawers open one by one and rummaged through them. No keys. I flung open his closet and searched for a key hook or anything a key might be stashed in. Nothing. I dug into the pockets of the three coats and two sweaters hanging there. I felt around on the floor. Still nothing.

I slammed the closet door shut and swore out loud, then quickly looked around to make sure no one had heard me.

What if he had it with him? What if he'd taken it home? We'd have no hope of getting hold of it then. Despairing, I slunk back to the outer office and dropped into Alice's chair. I could hear footsteps. She and Virginia were coming down the hall.

"Damn." I pounded my fist on the desk in frustration. With the impact, I heard a little tinkling sound.

There, not six inches from my hand, a small ceramic dish held about a half dozen paper clips and two keys on a ring with a little cardboard tag. I turned the tag so I could read it. NYPD CASE #90413. It had the studio's name on it, along with the address of the Coney Island apartment and this notation: FRONT DOOR, CLOSET. Jimmy must have just returned the keys that morning. I started to pick them up, then fumbled them and yanked my hand back as the door swung open.

"Thanks, Alice," Virginia said as they strolled in. "I guess he must have changed his mind about breaking in." She shot me a questioning look. I nodded, ever so slightly, toward the dish. Alice was heading for her desk.

"Oh, look," Virginia said, pointing out the window. Alice turned. I grabbed the keys and shoved them into my pocket. "Never mind. I thought I saw him coming back."

"You kids go on," Alice said. "I got work to do. Outta my chair, if you please."

I jumped up. Virginia and I hustled out of there, then broke into a run once we were sure we were out of Alice's sight.

"You got it?" she said, stopping.

"Got 'em both." I handed them to her.

We looked at each other an instant, then we both said: "Let's go."

CHAPTER NINE

"Why are you afraid of your manager, Billy?"

Virginia and I had the subway car to ourselves, rumbling toward Coney Island. The question stumped me for a second. Then I realized why. "No one ever asked me that before," I said.

"No one else has noticed?"

I shook my head, thinking of all the times I'd wanted to complain to Roscoe about my latest bruise, all the times I'd come close to telling my dad everything. Something had always stopped me. At times, the way Roscoe gave Maureen these dark looks, I would have sworn he knew. If he'd ever prompted me in the least, I'd have spilled it all. But it was almost as if neither he nor my dad wanted to know. They just left it alone. Left me alone.

Virginia looked at me and waited. I couldn't think of any good reason not to answer.

"Maureen hits me sometimes. She throws things."

"Out of the blue?"

"No, I can usually see it coming. She gets mad when I don't get a part I audition for. Or if I talk too much. Or she doesn't like my manners. One time I put my elbows on the table at dinner and she turned the whole table over on me." I was surprised to feel my throat tightening. "There's hell to pay if I ask the wrong question or make a mistake on the set or do anything she doesn't like." I fought back the tears that were seeping into my eyes.

"She sounds like a maniac."

"Like when I tried out for *Donovan's Kid*. We thought I had the part in the bag." I was getting wound up now, talking faster to keep the sobs from starting. "Everything was going great. Then we read in *Daily Variety* that Jackie Cooper got the part because I had a slight Cockney accent. Nobody called to warn us. The first we knew of it was when we read the paper. And it was the second time I'd lost a part to him. Maureen went nuts. First she threw the paper at me. Then she screamed at me, all kinds of stuff about my parents and their damn accent. Then she grabbed me by the arm and smacked me a few times."

"Oh, Billy," Virginia breathed.

"She does that kind of stuff all the time. I learned pretty quick to run for my room when she gets going."

"How can you stand it?" She looked like she might start crying, too.

"Sometimes I can't. One time I tried to bail out. I'd spent the weekend with my parents in New Bedford, and some of my cousins came down from Canada, and we all had a swell time together. Then my dad put me on the train Sunday because I had a rehearsal Monday afternoon. I cried as soon as he left. I just didn't think I could face New York again. So when the train stopped in Westerly, I got off."

"Didn't anyone see you?"

"Sure. I had to sweet-talk the conductor some. But he let me go. I spent the afternoon playing cards with these girls who worked at the magazine stand in the train station. Then my dad showed up. I guess the conductor told someone at the station to call him. And he drove me to the rehearsal hall the next day. Maureen puts on this deeply concerned face and says, 'Thank you, Mr. O'Dwyer. We were so worried about him.' That night, she beat the daylights out of me."

"Oh, Billy!"

For a couple of minutes, we both just sat, bracing ourselves when the subway car took a turn and letting the rattle and roar cover the sounds of our sniffling. I felt drained. "What about you?" I said at last, to change the subject. "Why don't you live with your parents?"

"They're in Europe. My father teaches at the University of Munich." She paused. "Aunt Trudi's all right. If you like boiled potatoes and sauerkraut. She cooks those a lot. My dad's brother was the cook in the family, but he died a few years ago. My dad's paying Aunt Trudi for my room and board. She needed money, and I needed to stay in New York for my career. So it works for everyone." Virginia didn't sound like it was working all that well for her, but I let it drop.

The train squealed into a station.

"So," I ventured, casting about for another conversation topic, "what do you think we'll find in that closet?"

She gave me that familiar Virginia look, and I began to feel better. As long as I had Virginia looking at me like I was an idiot, things were all right.

"Well," she said, "if we get off this train before the doors close, we might find out."

I looked out the window. She was right, as usual. This was our stop.

We let ourselves into the apartment and stood before the closet, barely breathing. Virginia held the key ring in front of her. Over it, she looked at me meaningfully. For a change, I was the one to roll eyeballs. "Can we just get on with it?" I said.

She made a little "hmph" sound and pushed the key into the closet doorknob. Slowly, melodramatically, she turned the knob and pulled the door open.

I looked in and gasped. "Oh, my gosh! Coats! Galoshes! In an entryway closet! Definitely some important clues here."

"Are you finished?" she said. "I'd like to get to work."

She first looked through the four winter coats that hung there, digging shocking items out of the pockets, like chewing gum wrappers, racetrack tickets, and a shopping list. We could see a couple of tennis rackets and some hats on the shelf above the coats. But we would have needed a stool to reach these, so we went for the floor first. Virginia pulled out the galoshes and a pair of what looked like expensive, but old, men's shoes. She looked inside them, like she might find a note from the killer or something, then set them aside.

"Have a look through these." She handed me a pair of leather-bound books.

I sat on the floor and opened the first one while she worked on climbing up to see the stuff on the shelf. On the first page in big letters were the words HARKIN STUDIOS, just like they looked on the sign at the gate. Below that, in smaller type, 1931. I turned the page and saw that it was a ledger. I'm no accountant, but I'd seen the household records my Auntie Annie kept. She was real particular about that kind of thing. The pages in the ledger book looked a lot like my aunt's accounts, only more complicated. I could make out some of it, though.

There were entries about payments to people I knew—the stage crew, a couple of actors, and so on—and some that apparently concerned bills for power, water, catering, things like that. I could see that some entries showed income, but I couldn't puzzle out the sources.

"This is just a studio account book for last year," I said. "No secret messages from the killer." I closed the book and handed it back to Virginia, who of course was not about to take my word for anything. She sat down and started turning pages as I picked up the other volume.

The second ledger book was thinner. It, too, had HARKIN STUDIOS on the first page, along with OFFICE—1931. Some of the entries made no sense to me, but others were pretty clear.

"This must be Mr. Harkin's own account," I said. "Look here. He's paid for haircuts, shoe shines, breakfast." I was fascinated to see how much money he spent on these everyday kinds of expenses. Every few pages there was an income entry of five thousand dollars, noted as S.A., with a little star in front of it. I pointed them out to Virginia. "What do you think these mean?"

She frowned. "No idea. Are there a lot of them?"

I looked more carefully. They appeared every Friday, with only a few breaks.

"They're weekly," I said. "Oh, I know. S.A., 'Studio Account.' There are payments like this in the other one to 'O.A.' That must mean 'Office Account.'"

"There are?" She flipped back through some pages, her face going a little pink. Miss Detective had actually missed something.

"Can't ignore a clue like that, can we?" I tried not to gloat too conspicuously—especially since I didn't really think those numbers were a clue to anything.

She shot me a dark look but didn't comment. We went back through both books, comparing entries on those Fridays.

"This makes sense," she said. "He took money from the studio's regular account and put it into his office account—"

"So he could pay for those twenty-dollar haircuts," I said.

"And paper clips, I'm sure. And probably Alice's salary."

I sat back, the small ledger in my lap, and kept turning pages. "You know, I think this is his handwriting."

"How do you know?"

"I have this note he wrote me after my last picture, saying how much he liked it. Who'd have thought a big boss like Mr. Harkin would do his own books?" It looked to me like he hadn't done a very good job of it. I nudged Virginia. "Look, here's a Friday where he made an entry putting the five thousand dollars into the office account, but then he forgot to carry it over to Monday. I bet an accountant would get fired for a mistake like that."

"Mr. Harkin can run a studio but can't manage something that simple?" She leaned over and looked at the office ledger. We checked more Fridays. He hadn't made the error only once. It was that way every weekend. As the year went on, the amounts got bigger: ten thousand, twenty thousand, twenty-five thousand. Each time the money was shown going into the office account on Friday, it was gone on Monday.

She looked at me with an excitement in her eyes that was scary. "That money is getting spent every weekend. Where could it be going?" She took the ledger from me and began leafing through it from the beginning, examining each page. "Here's a clue, in April. After the five thousand dollars comes in on this Friday there's a five thousand dollar payment to 'Cash—J. M.'"

"Aren't we getting a little off the track here?" I asked, exasperated. "What difference does it make where the money goes? None of this has anything to do with Amelia."

"How do we know that?"

I almost felt sorry for her, she sounded so desperate to figure out this new mystery.

"Besides," she continued, "what else do we have to go on? I just have a feeling—why are these books even here? In an apartment closet away from the studio? And we don't know why Amelia was here, either. . . ."

"And that makes the books and Amelia connected?" I hated to keep shooting down her theories, but they were getting dumber by the minute.

"Just think, please," she said. "Do you know of anything Mr. Harkin does almost every weekend that could cost this much?"

I thought. "No. I have no idea what he does on weekends. He probably goes to the studio parties, like everyone else. I've seen him at a few."

"Parties? What are they like?"

"Boring. I hate them. I have to be clever and polite, like a nice little star. The only good thing about them is that Maureen takes me home before everyone gets too stinking drunk."

"There's alcohol at the parties? That's illegal."

I reminded myself that Virginia hadn't been around these people for two years like I had.

"It doesn't matter if it's illegal. These are movie people. They can do whatever they want. You think the cops care? Jimmy Mandell's always there guarding the door, wearing his shiny Italian loafers instead of those cop shoes."

She frowned, still turning ledger pages. Suddenly she stopped. "Look at this, Billy. A page has been ripped out here, between a Friday and a Monday."

"Yeah, I know," I said. "I saw some other places like that."

She slapped her forehead. "Billy O'Dwyer, how can you look right at a clue like this and miss it?" She was flipping from week to week now, looking closely into the book's binding after each Friday page. "They've all been torn out. Every weekend page, every week that the money is moved to the office account and disappears by Monday. Someone has gotten rid of the pages that must say where the money was going. Don't you get it?"

"No."

"Then see if you can answer this: Jimmy Mandell works in Flatbush, where the studio is. Why was he the first cop to arrive at a murder scene in Coney Island?"

"I never thought of that," I said. Suddenly, everything clicked into place. "How about that. You did it, Virginia. You solved the case."

"*We* did it," she said, grinning. We closed the ledgers and stood up. I handed her the fatter one, and she hugged them both. "Let's take these to Mr. Harkin. We can't give Jimmy the chance to get rid of any more evidence."

"Yeah," I said. "He probably thought no one would notice those pages he tore out. We'll have Roscoe out of jail by dinnertime—if the D.A. hasn't already set him free. I am really glad to have this over."

We shook on it, our partners—shake, just like when we'd started the case. Then we returned everything else to the way we'd found it and left.

It was getting late, so we ran all the way to the subway. After this day of triumph, I didn't need to have Maureen get to the studio and find me not there. In front of the station, a kid was hawking newspapers. His shouts made us freeze in our tracks.

"Extry, extry, read all about it! Chubby Muldoon trial to start Monday! Prosecutor says he's got the evidence to send comedian to the electric chair! Extry, extry!"

CHAPTER TEN

It was all I could do to keep from snatching the newspaper out of Maureen's hands that night. When she finally set it down, I got my first chance to learn what the district attorney was feeling so cocky about. Somehow, he had twisted what Mr. Harkin had said about Roscoe and Amelia and had come to the ridiculous conclusion that Roscoe had been trying to romance Amelia and she had turned him down.

"In a fit of rage," the *Post* reported, "the spurned Mr. Muldoon brutally beat his costar to death."

I felt awful for Mr. Harkin. He must be

blaming himself for this terrible turn of events, and after he'd done his best to get Roscoe freed in a hurry. I was sure he'd be happy to hear that Virginia and I had cracked the case—happy enough to forgive us for sneaking off the studio grounds. Swiping his keys and sneaking off the grounds. Swiping the keys, sneaking out, breaking into his locked closet, rooting through his private records, and taking his ledger books. Okay, so he would have to very, *very* happy to forgive all that. But I was sure he would be.

Virginia brought the ledger books to the studio the next morning. We'd figured it would be much easier—and considerably less dangerous—for her to conceal the books from her aunt than for me to try to keep Maureen from noticing them.

When Virginia's aunt and Maureen finally left us on our own, we dropped our public smiles. I felt like my face would crack.

"Have you seen Mr. Harkin yet?" Virginia asked.

"No, but he doesn't always come through the soundstage in the morning," I said. "There's another entrance on the office side."

"Let's go."

She carried the books, and we walked as nonchalantly as we could, across the soundstage, veering clear of any early morning crew members who might want to chat or ask questions. But we hadn't gone far when Virginia, who was in the lead, stopped suddenly. I crashed into her.

"Hey——" I began.

She grabbed my wrist, her eyes wide. Then I saw what she was looking at.

Not twenty feet away, Jimmy Mandell stood talking to the sound guy.

Virginia whirled me around and we scurried—nonchalantly, of course—back to the little group of stools and tables where everyone parked their things.

"He knows," she said. "He knows we took them."

"Calm down, Virginia. How could he know?"

"We can't walk past him with these books."

"Leave them here," I suggested. "Where's the rest of your stuff? Just slide them under your script and pile your sweater on top. No one will notice them. We can tell Mr. Harkin about the torn pages and what we figured out. He'll know what to do."

"I'm scared, Billy."

"Jimmy can't do anything to us here. This is our place, not his. We've got friends all around us. Just

94 **EILEEN HEYES**

look." I swept an arm toward the cameras, the light trees, the set. . . . Actually, there weren't all that many people around at this hour, since there was no movie in production this week. "Look, we'll just hold our heads up, act innocent, and walk past him. Okay?"

"Okay," she said.

For a scared girl, she sure recovered fast. As we passed Jimmy, she called out a pleasant "good morning" to him. I almost choked on my own fear.

We headed down the hall toward Mr. Harkin's office.

"He's not going to like this," she stage-whispered.

"Sure, he will," I whispered back. "Why wouldn't he?"

"Because in order to clear Roscoe, he'll have to admit he was bribing a cop. That's a crime, Billy."

"Yeah, but everyone pays off the cops. You don't see anyone going to jail for that, do you?"

We found Mr. Harkin alone in his office. Alice hadn't come in yet. We tapped at the door, which was halfway open.

"Yes?"

I pushed through the doorway. The boss was sitting at his desk.

"Hiya, Mr. Harkin. Can we talk to you?"

"Oh, good morning, Billy. Good morning, ah—"

"Virginia," she prompted.

"Virginia," Mr. Harkin said. "I don't have a lot of time this morning. What can I do for you kids?"

While I tried to decide where to start, my partner and mouthpiece piped up.

"We've found out who really killed Amelia St. Augustine, and we know why he did it," Virginia announced, all trace of quaver gone from her voice.

"Have you?" Mr. Harkin sounded doubtful. He walked over and shut the door.

"Yes. We have evidence that will make Roscoe Muldoon a free man."

Mr. Harkin returned to his desk. "And what evidence is that?"

"Mr. Harkin," I cut in, "there are a few things we need to explain first —"

"We found your ledger books in the closet at Roscoe's apartment," Virginia charged on. "We know about the money that was moved from the studio account to your office account on Fridays and then disappeared. And we know where the money went."

Mr. Harkin paled. "How did you kids get into that closet?"

"That's what I wanted to explain," I began.

"And where are those ledgers now?"

"We have them here. Including the one Jimmy Mandell tore pages out of to hide what was going on,"Virginia finished, looking quite triumphant.

"Where are they?" Mr. Harkin repeated.

"With my things out on the soundstage," Virginia said. "Jimmy's out there now poking around, and we didn't want him to catch us with them."

"Mr. Harkin," I said, "I know you don't want all this to come out in public, but I don't think you have anything to worry about with the D.A. I mean, when he's got a killer in his hands, don't you think he'll overlook a few bribes to a cop?"

Mr. Harkin looked confused for a second. He opened his mouth, then shut it without speaking. His face relaxed a bit, and he raised an eyebrow. I could tell he was impressed that we had puzzled out the whole story. "Go get the books," he said. "Bring them here."

Virginia and I started for the door.

"No, wait," Mr. Harkin said. "We shouldn't talk about this here, not with Jimmy so close. There's no telling what he'll do. A desperate man like Jimmy. I'll tell you what. Billy, do you remember that clubhouse from *Play Ball*? Do you know where we moved it to?"

"Sure. It's out behind Soundstage Thirteen, with all that other spare scenery and stuff."

"Right. You kids get the ledgers and meet me at the clubhouse in, oh, fifteen minutes. Don't let Jimmy see you. Okay?"

"Got it," I said.

"Good," Mr. Harkin said. "I'll see you there."

We hurried back to the soundstage, where Jimmy was nowhere in sight. Virginia grabbed the ledgers, and we headed out across the studio property.

Soundstage Thirteen was at the far corner of the lot. It hadn't been used in some time, since the studio had cut back production because of the Depression. When we reached the clubhouse, we had to shove a couple of scenery flats and a heavy barrel out of the way to get the door open. Remnants of some Western, I figured. Maybe one of Lance Williams's pictures.

The building was supposed to have been a garage that we kids had fixed up for our gang. It was made of wood, roof shingles and all, with cracks between the slats in the walls and a couple of small windows through which we'd thrown tomatoes at Denny Carlisle. The windows were boarded up now, and the clubhouse had some old wagon wheels, a rack of costumes, a few lasso ropes, a bunch of chairs, and some other props stored in it.

We pulled the door closed and sat in the dusty darkness, waiting. After what seemed like only a few moments we heard footsteps come up to the door. I dashed over and shoved it open to let Mr. Harkin in. Then I froze.

Standing there, his bulk blocking the daylight, was Jimmy Mandell.

I tried to yank the door closed, but he slipped through it too fast. I backed up, staring at him, unable to speak.

"You kids wouldn't listen to me, would you?" he said, his manicured fingers tapping the revolver at his hip. "You had to keep poking your noses in where they didn't belong. Had to play detective." He took another step toward us.

"We know everything, Jimmy," my partner shot back. "And we told it all to Mr. Harkin. You won't get away with it."

"And what is it that you're thinking I want to get away with?" He looked genuinely curious. The guy should have been an actor. In fact, at that moment, I wished he were *anything* other than an armed cop.

"The murder of Amelia St. Augustine," Virginia said. She held up the ledger books. "We've got the proof right here."

He shook his head and sighed. "You kids don't know what you're talking about."

At last, I found my voice. "Yes, we do," I said. "Amelia hated booze. You worked at all the studio parties, not enforcing the law but making sure it was safe for everyone to drink like fish. And why wouldn't a cop tell the Prohibition Bureau about the people who supplied all that liquor? Because he was lining his own pockets with the studio's money in exchange for keeping his trap shut."

"Amelia found out you were getting paid off for your silence," Virginia said, continuing to spin out our deductions. "She found out Mr. Harkin kept records, and she found out where those records were."

"Records?" Jimmy said. "There weren't no records."

"Don't you wish," Virginia snapped, so sassy that you'd have thought she was the one with the gun on her hip.

"Amelia used to live in that apartment in Coney Island," I went on. "She still had her key. So she went over there last Wednesday to collect these ledger books." I pointed at the volumes in Virginia's hands. "She was going to turn you in."

"And you couldn't have that, could you?" Virginia said. "You found out what she had in mind, and you followed her. And then you killed her, right there in Roscoe's living room."

"And made up that phony baloney story about the call from the downstairs neighbor with the accent," I said. "There isn't any downstairs neighbor. And there wasn't any call."

"Hold it—" Jimmy began.

"Why did Mr. Harkin keep paying you bigger and bigger amounts?" Virginia asked. "Were you blackmailing him? Threatening to actually enforce the law?"

To my enormous relief, he took his hand away from that revolver and folded his arms in front of him. "So you got it all figured out, have you?" he said, cocking his head.

"That's right," Virginia answered. "So you may as well give yourself up. It'll go easier for you if you do."

I shot her a look. Where did she come up with this kind of stuff?

"Well, you got it wrong," Jimmy said. "I didn't kill her. And I did get that call. I tried to tell the guy to call the Coney Island precinct, but he said I should be the one to go. Said he knew I worked for the studio, and this trouble involved one of the studio's biggest stars. So I went."

"Nice try," I said.

"Tell it to the judge," Virginia added. Jeez, she can be corny.

"All right, kids, the game is over," Jimmy said. "Come on, let's go."

Just then, I saw a shadow outside the door. I nudged Virginia and signaled with a lift of my chin.

Jimmy caught my gesture and whirled away from us just as Mr. Harkin lunged in. He grabbed for Jimmy's gun, but Jimmy was too quick and twisted out of his reach. Mr. Harkin stumbled, then caught his balance in an instant. He grabbed the gun handle, and the two of them struggled for endless seconds.

I hit the floor and crouched close up behind Jimmy's legs. Mr. Harkin got the picture. Keeping a grip on the gun, he shoved Jimmy backward. Jimmy tumbled over me and landed hard.

I stood up. My back ached, but relief flooded through me. Barely able to keep my knees from buckling, I stepped beside Mr. Harkin. Virginia joined us. Even in the dim light, I could see she was pale. I understood. Fear had kept us strong; relief left us weak.

"Thanks, Mr. Harkin," I said. "You got here just in time."

"Seems that way," he said. "So you figured out that Jimmy killed Amelia over booze and bribes, eh?"

"You heard?" Virginia asked.

"I heard. And what about your evidence? In the ledger books?"

Jimmy remained on the floor, half-sitting, breathing hard and staring daggers at Mr. Harkin.

"He tore out pages from the office ledger," I said. "The pages that showed you were paying him thousands of dollars nearly every week."

Mr. Harkin motioned with the gun. "Billy, Virginia, grab that lasso rope over there. Tie him up. We don't want to give him any chance to escape."

Virginia set the ledgers down on the floor while I fetched the rope. Lasso rope isn't great for tying knots, but we did the best we could. Within minutes we had Jimmy trussed, more or less. She grabbed the books again.

Mr. Harkin pulled a handkerchief out of his pocket and shoved it into Jimmy's mouth. "There," he said, sounding satisfied. "Now pull those hand-cuffs out of his belt."

Jimmy's eyes widened, and he tried to object, but he was in no position to tell us what to do. I grabbed the cuffs.

"So you figured out that Jimmy killed Amelia, huh?" Mr. Harkin said again.

"Yup," I said.

"But somehow he got wind of your discoveries."

"I don't know how——"

"And he lured you out here to this old shed."

"No, Mr. Harkin," I said. "Remember? You just told us—"

"You confronted him with your evidence. But he got the drop on you and handcuffed you to that wheel." He waved the gun toward a wagon wheel that leaned against the wall across the clubhouse from where Jimmy lay.

"What?" I said. "He never did that." I looked at Virginia, who was staring at Mr. Harkin.

"Then you do it," Mr. Harkin said.

Finally I got it. Man, did I get it.

"Go on," he said, raising the gun toward us. "Go handcuff yourselves to that wheel. Put it around one of the spokes and on both your wrists."

Like we couldn't have figured that out. Virginia clutched the ledgers with one hand while I put the cuffs on her other wrist and on mine.

"And then, Jimmy figured he couldn't let you walk around with the evidence that was going to put him away. So he decided to burn the evidence and take care of two snoopy kids at the same time. Unfortunately for him, he got caught in his own trap." Mr. Harkin pulled some papers from a pocket inside his jacket and unfolded them. "He started the fire with these very ledger pages, the ones he tore out of the book."

Mr. Harkin set the pages down on top of a crate, struck a match, and lit them. "And he had to make sure those books were destroyed, too. Let me have them." He walked over and reached toward Virginia.

She hugged them to herself.

"I don't understand, Mr. Harkin," I said hastily. "Why'd you do it? Why'd you kill Amelia?"

As I'd hoped, he stopped. Behind him, Jimmy shifted his weight. Smoke rose from the burning pages, its acrid smell making my nostrils tingle. I watched Mr. Harkin's face.

"Your theory was partly right," he said, "but mostly wrong. I didn't kill Amelia. It was an accident. She had the office ledger, and I tried to get it away from her, but she wouldn't let the thing go. She fell and hit her head on the coffee table."

I could see out of the corner of my eye that Virginia, too, was looking at Mr. Harkin but watching something else.

"Well, if it was an accident," I said, "why didn't you just tell the cops that?"

"Kid, you're asking too many questions."

Smoke collected under the ceiling. A flame from the burning papers licked up toward the costume rack a foot away. Suddenly Virginia turned on me. "Billy O'Dwyer, this is all your fault!" she yelled. "You got us into this stupid mess."

I hesitated only a beat. "Me?" I shouted back. "It was your cockamamie idea to go play detective, not mine. Now look what you've gotten us into."

"I'm so mad, I could just kick you!"

Mr. Harkin pursed his lips, watching us bicker.

"Try it, and see if I don't kick you right back," I said. I could see her silently count: One. Two. On three, we both turned toward Mr. Harkin and kicked hard. I got him in the kneecap. Virginia's foot flew higher and whacked the gun from his hand. It landed about two feet away from Jimmy, who was squirming out of the stiff rope we'd tried to tie him with. He pulled the gag out of his mouth.

While Mr. Harkin collapsed to his knees, shouting curses I will not repeat, Jimmy grabbed the gun and got to his feet.

At that moment, flames shot up the arm of a hanging costume. The whole rack was in blazes within seconds.

Jimmy holstered the gun, hurried to us, and unlocked the cuffs. "Come on, kids, let's get out of here."

"Wait," Virginia said as I started to hustle toward the door. "What about Mr. Harkin?"

"Don't worry," Jimmy said. "I won't leave him here. He's got a story he needs to tell some people." While Virginia and I coughed on smoke, Jimmy managed to twist Mr. Harkin's arms behind him and put the handcuffs on his wrists.

Flames had reached the roof of the clubhouse. Fire flashed over our heads.

"Let's get out," I yelled. "Now!"

We stumbled around the blazing props and out the door. I could feel the heat on my back as the roof crashed in behind us.

CHAPTER ELEVEN

Late that afternoon, six of us sat in a small conference room at the police precinct: Virginia, her Aunt Trudi, Maureen, Roscoe, my dad, and me. Jimmy Mandell walked in with a file folder under one arm. I noticed the gold ring was absent from his pinkie. He nodded to Roscoe, introduced himself to the other adults and shook hands all around, then sat down behind the table in the middle of the room.

"These are some spunky kids you folks got here," he said. Virginia and I grinned at each other. "So. Have you figured out the rest of the story?"

"Some of it," I said. "But if Mr. Harkin and Amelia weren't arguing over booze, what did she find in the ledger book that he wanted to keep secret?"

"He was losing the studio's money at the track. Lots of the studio's money. He thought he was borrowing it, just to go out and recoup his losses. He meant to pay it back—and I believe that. He bet real safe, always playing favorites."

My dad snorted. "Damn favorites have been costing me, too."

"He kept records in that ledger of what he lost at the track?" I said.

"Real careful records," Jimmy said.

I remembered Dad telling me what a good year it had been for long-shot horses. Then other things came back to me. The racetrack tickets in Mr. Harkin's coat pocket. The newspaper stories about the studio not paying its bills. Lance Williams saying that Mr. Harkin had to watch every dime, and that the actors were looking for a lifeboat. They had known the studio was sinking.

"It was about gambling," Virginia said, speaking my own thought before I could get the words out.

"Amelia hated gambling as much as she hated alcohol, because of her father. Rachel told us, Billy, remember?"

I nodded. "But how did Amelia get into the closet if Mr. Harkin didn't want her to?"

"She had her own key," Jimmy said. "She was the one who had the lock put on the closet in the first place, back when she lived there and wanted to keep her fancy furs locked up. After she moved out, Harkin started stashing some of his old things there. When he took those ledgers away from the studio, he figured that closet full of junk was the perfect hiding place."

I recalled something else. "One page of the office ledger showed he'd taken cash out for a 'J. M.'" I gulped. "For you?"

A quick, grim smile crossed Jimmy's face. "Like I told you, there weren't no records of him paying me anything. That was the cash he took out for his trips to the racetrack. Joseph M. Harkin—his own initials. He must have missed that one when he was tearing out pages. Harkin was a gambler, but he wasn't no thief. At least, he didn't set out to be one. Or a killer, neither."

"But he ended up being both," Virginia said.

"The studio's been having big money trouble," I said, still assembling the pieces in my mind, "because Mr. Harkin was draining the studio's account to play the horses."

"And on top of that," Roscoe said, "I was about to leave and take along the stars that were making enough money to keep Harkin Studios in business."

"Oh?" Jimmy said. "I didn't know that part. Well, that explains a few things, too."

"Clue us in, will you?" It was the first time Maureen had spoken since we'd all gone into the conference room.

"Think about it," Jimmy said. "Miss St. Augustine tells him she's gonna get that book and tell everyone what he's been up to. He goes after her, to the apartment."

I remembered Mr. Harkin striding across the soundstage the morning it happened, too distracted to answer the greetings called to him from all directions. He'd been on his way to Coney Island.

"They struggle, she falls and hits her head," Jimmy continued. "Now he's got a dead actress on the floor of an apartment that's occupied by a man who's been causing him headaches. He knows Mr. Muldoon will be bringing home his case of bootleg soon—everyone knew what Mr. Muldoon did on Wednesdays."

"He figured he could solve two problems at the same time," Virginia said. "Amelia was out of his way. And if the world thought Roscoe killed her, that would get Roscoe out of his hair, too."

"He's the one who called you," I said to Jimmy. "The guy with the accent. It wasn't Russian or Hungarian. It was Polish, the accent he learned from his parents." I turned to Roscoe. "Jeez, and I thought Mr. Harkin was trying to help you. But that press conference two days ago—he knew exactly how the D.A. would react. He meant to hand the D.A. a motive he could use."

Roscoe just nodded.

"That's right," Jimmy said. "He got real worried when it looked like the D.A.'s case was coming undone, so he fed all that blarney to the reporters about Mr. Muldoon and Miss St. Augustine going out together." He shook his head. "That's when I started thinking something was fishy."

"How did you happen to be at the clubhouse this morning?" I asked.

"I saw you two acting real sneaky and walking off the soundstage with them big books, and I had a bad feeling you were asking for trouble. I figured I'd better keep an eye on you, so I followed you."

"Officer Mandell, I can't thank you enough for rescuing these children." Maureen stood first, and the rest of us followed suit. She gave me and Virginia a fond look. I could tell I'd be in for it later. "Are we finished?"

"I think so for now, Mrs. Fritz. And you might be the last one to call me 'Officer Mandell.' I'm turning in my badge tonight."

"Why, Jimmy?" Virginia asked.

"I'm a small-town guy, miss. I tried to play this big-city game, but it's too rough for me. I can't work for people who'd try to save their careers by hurting kids."

"But won't you be in trouble for—" I felt Virginia's swift kick to my ankle.

"For taking payoffs?" Jimmy finished for me. "I doubt it. No one else ever is. And you didn't hear that from me." He studied his fingernails for a moment. "I'm gonna visit my parents in Fall River and just look in a mirror for a while, see what I've become. And then I think I'll try to become something better."

"You're from Fall River?" I said. "We're practically neighbors."

"That so?" He smiled, looking more relaxed than I'd ever seen him.

Maureen pushed her handbag strap over her arm. "Let's go home, Billy. I imagine the studio will shut down for a while, and heaven only knows what will happen with Mr. Harkin gone. But you and Virginia can use the next few weeks to work on some dance routines."

"I need a break," I blurted.

Maureen turned to me. "You need what?" She lost her fond look for only a moment—but it must have been long enough for both Roscoe and my dad to see.

"He said he needs a break," Roscoe said, his glare challenging her to argue. She opened her mouth for an instant, then snapped it shut. Roscoe's face softened as he looked at me. "Pardner, you stuck up for me when I needed it. From now on, I'm sticking up for you, too." He shot Maureen another hard look. "Count on it."

"I'm taking Billy home to New Bedford for a while," my dad said, uncertainty in his eyes as they flicked from Roscoe to Maureen. "Get him some rest. We'll call you soon, Maureen."

I threw my arms around him, fighting back tears. "Can I come?"

We turned and stared at Virginia.

"I could use some time out of the city, too. Can I go visit Billy's family, Aunt Trudi? Please?"

I wanted to hug her, too. I liked the idea of having her around while I got used to being home again.

"If it's all right with Mr. O'Dwyer," her aunt said.

"We'd be happy to have you," Dad told Virginia. "You two kids have been through a lot together this past week."

With that, our little group broke up.

An hour later, Dad, Virginia, and I all sat in the front seat of his Whippet on the way home to New Bedford. I thought about that first day I'd met Maureen at my dad's golf course, how his face had lit up at the thought of his kid being in pictures.

And I thought about Leon riding his bike, the way I never got a chance to, and how I'd been ready to fight him for one little spin. I remembered all the encouragement my dad had given me every time he sent me back to New York, while my mother had just cried. How he'd driven me all the way to rehearsal after I'd jumped the train in Rhode Island that one time, not even asking me why I was so desperate to avoid going back.

My dad, my hero in all the world, kept smiling, kept telling me to keep my chin up, kept sending me back.

I knew that before the day was over, I would have to show him my bruises and tell him the truth. What would happen after that, I didn't know.

I turned to see Virginia gazing out the window, riding some private thought off past the horizon. And I knew that, as many times as she had rescued me in the past week, this time I would have to go it alone.

I took a deep breath. "Dad?"

"Yes, Billy?"

"When we get home, there's something I have to talk to you about."

He glanced at me and was silent for a moment. Then he said simply, "Sure, son."

Dad reached down and squeezed my hand as the car rumbled up the highway toward Massachusetts, toward my family and my home.

DEAR READER:

I come from several generations of spotlight seekers. My great-grandfather was an Irish clog dancer. My grandfather traveled all over Europe as a dancer and comedian in Vaudeville shows. My father was in movies when he was a kid. I thought for a while that I, too, would become a performer. But the hermit-like existence of a writer is more my style.

When I was growing up, I used to listen to my father's stories about his life in the movies. Everywhere he went, people recognized him and asked for his autograph. He had to live in New York City with his manager, a quick-tempered woman who beat him for the smallest goof. He didn't tell his parents about the way this woman treated him—not until years later, when she had long since passed from their lives.

Nothing about his stories struck me as odd. I assumed everyone's parents had made movies and been beaten as children. As I grew older it dawned on me that my dad's past was unusual. But only when I had sons of my own did I begin to comprehend what it must have been like to be in my father's position: wanting to do something he loved, knowing he had to earn money to support his family, and knowing, too, that he must keep secret the violence in his life. All this for two years, starting when he was only seven.

Thus was born the character of Billy O'Dwyer.

The year *Acting Innocent* takes place—1932—was a difficult one for Americans. A Constitutional amendment had made it illegal to make or sell alcoholic drinks since 1920, a law known as Prohibition. But the law didn't stop Americans from drinking. It just turned normally law-abiding people into criminals. The country was also suffering the effects of the Great Depression, a time when many businesses closed and millions of people lost their jobs and homes. My grandparents—in this book, Billy's parents—were among those millions.

I salute the strength and spunk and spirit of my parents and all those of their generation who figured out how to still be kids. Through all the hard times, they somehow managed to keep acting innocent.

Eileen Heyes